This Little Tiger book belongs to:

_____

_____

_____

For my mum
~ D B
For Andy, Caroline,
Charlotte and Harry
~ T W

LITTLE TIGER PRESS
An imprint of Magi Publications
1 The Coda Centre, 189 Munster Road, London SW6 6AW
www.littletigerpress.com

First published in Great Britain 2005
This edition published 2005

Text copyright © David Bedford 2005
Illustrations copyright © Tim Warnes 2005
David Bedford and Tim Warnes have asserted their rights
to be identified as the author and illustrator of this work
under the Copyright, Designs and Patents Act, 1988

A CIP catalogue record for this book is available
from the British Library

All rights reserved • ISBN 1 84506 195 0

Printed in Belgium by Proost N.V.

2 4 6 8 10 9 7 5 3 1

I've Seen Santa!

David Bedford

Illustrated by
Tim Warnes

LITTLE TIGER PRESS
London

It was Christmas Eve and Little Bear was looking forward to seeing Santa.

"Is Santa as big as you?" he asked Big Bear.

"Nearly," said Big Bear, proudly.

"Oh," said Little Bear, looking worried.
"Will Santa fit down our chimney, then?"
    "Of course he will!" said Big Bear. "I'll show you."
    Big Bear went outside and climbed into
the chimney . . .

CRASH!

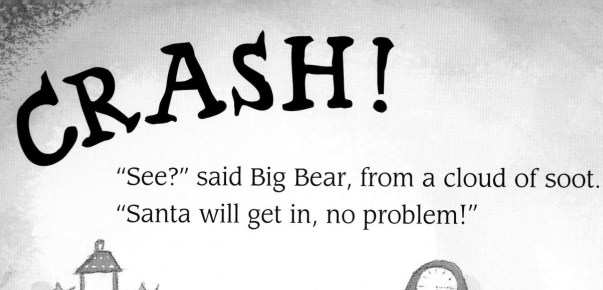

"See?" said Big Bear, from a cloud of soot.
"Santa will get in, no problem!"

"Santa won't come if he sees this mess!"
said Mummy Bear.
"We'll help clean up," said Little Bear.

"Does Santa visit bears
all over the world?"
said Little Bear.
    "Yes," said Big Bear.
"He goes to every
    house."

"Hmm," said Little Bear. "He might not have time to come here, and then I won't have any presents."
"Don't worry," said Mummy Bear. "Santa will come just as soon as you go to sleep."

For SANTA
(paws OFF, Big Bear)

Little Bear didn't want to go to sleep.
He wanted to see Santa. He listened to
Mummy Bear and Big Bear going to bed.
And then . . . GLUG, GLUG, GLUG, GLUG!

What was that noise?
Someone was downstairs!

Someone big was sitting
in the fireplace.
"Yes!" whispered Little Bear.
"It's Santa! I've seen Santa!"
Little Bear tiptoed up and saw . . .

. . . Big Bear!

"That's Santa's milk!" said Little Bear.
"I only wanted a sip," said Big Bear,
"before I go to sleep." He took Little
Bear's hand. "Come on, Little Bear.
Let's go to bed."

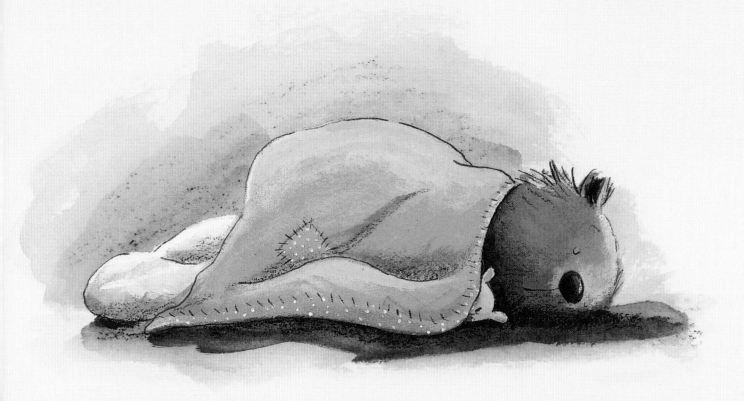

Little Bear tried to stay awake, but he soon fell into a doze.

Then a loud noise downstairs woke him up.

MUNCH! MUNCH! MUNCH! MUNCH!

Someone big was
standing by the
Christmas tree.
This time it had to be . . .

. . . Big Bear again!

"You're eating Santa's mince
pies now!" said Little Bear.
      "I was hungry," said Big Bear.

"If Santa's as greedy as you,"
said Mummy Bear, coming
downstairs, "he'll be too big
and he WILL get stuck in the
chimney! Now go to bed
and go to sleep –
both of you!"

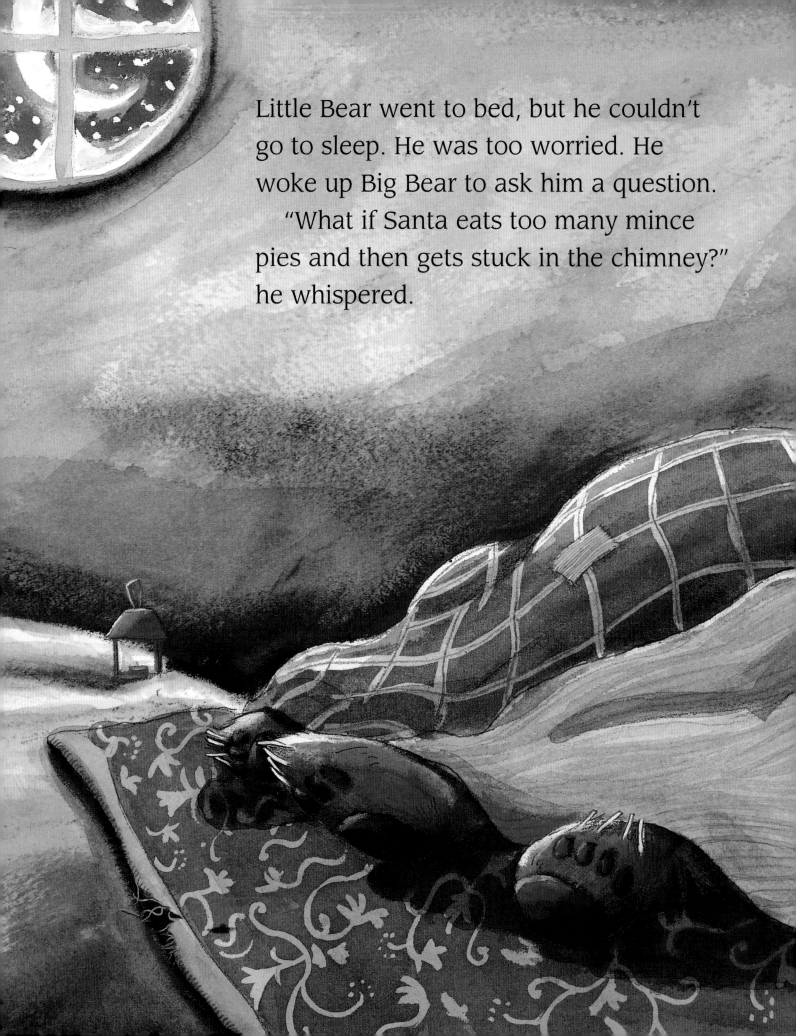

Little Bear went to bed, but he couldn't go to sleep. He was too worried. He woke up Big Bear to ask him a question.
"What if Santa eats too many mince pies and then gets stuck in the chimney?" he whispered.

"Hmm," said Big Bear.

"Let's keep watch to make sure he's OK," said Little Bear. "We can hide so he won't see us."

"Shhh!" whispered Little Bear
from their hiding place.
"I can hear something!
It MUST be Santa this time!"

Someone was putting
presents in their stockings!
Big Bear turned on his
torch to see . . .

. . . Mummy Bear!

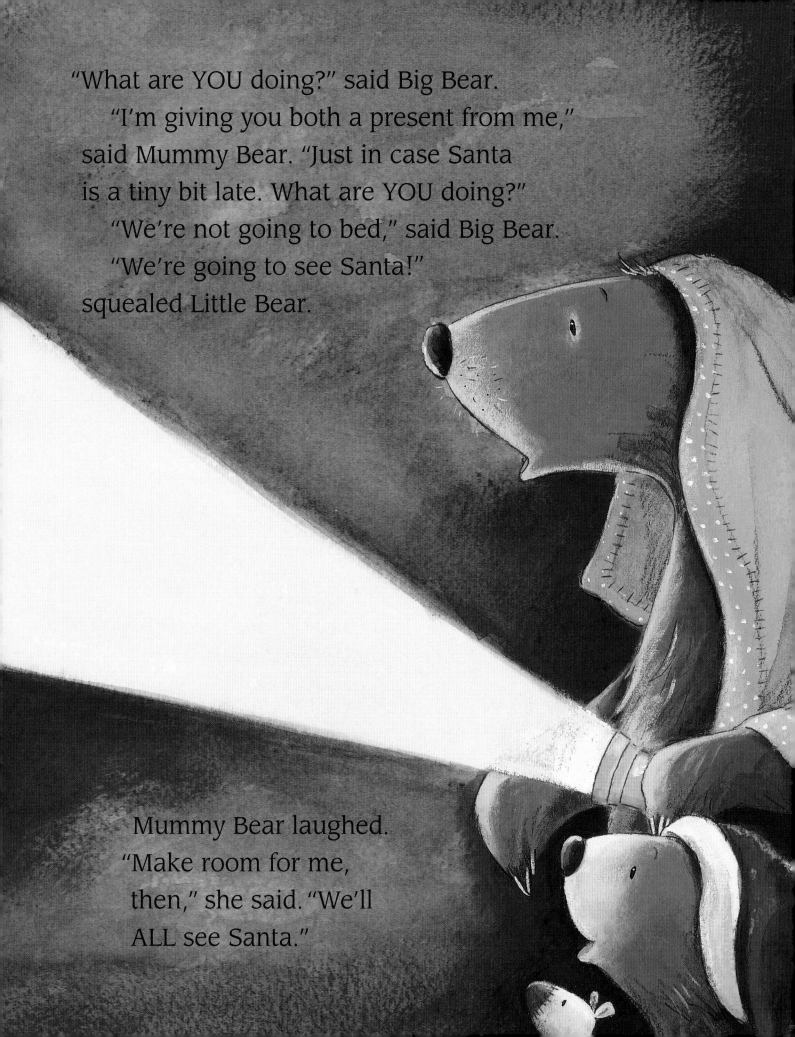

"What are YOU doing?" said Big Bear.

"I'm giving you both a present from me,"
said Mummy Bear. "Just in case Santa
is a tiny bit late. What are YOU doing?"

"We're not going to bed," said Big Bear.

"We're going to see Santa!"
squealed Little Bear.

Mummy Bear laughed.
"Make room for me,
then," she said. "We'll
ALL see Santa."

Little Bear, Big Bear and
Mummy Bear stayed downstairs
all through the night.

But they never did see Santa . . .

. . . even though
Santa saw them!

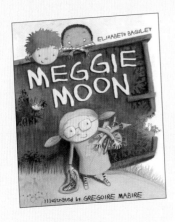  

Perfect presents
from Little Tiger Press

  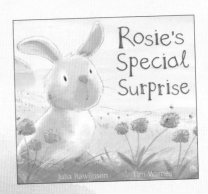

For information regarding any of the above titles or for our catalogue, please contact us:
Little Tiger Press, 1 The Coda Centre, 189 Munster Road, London SW6 6AW
Tel: 020 7385 6333 Fax: 020 7385 7333 E-mail: info@littletiger.co.uk www.littletigerpress.com

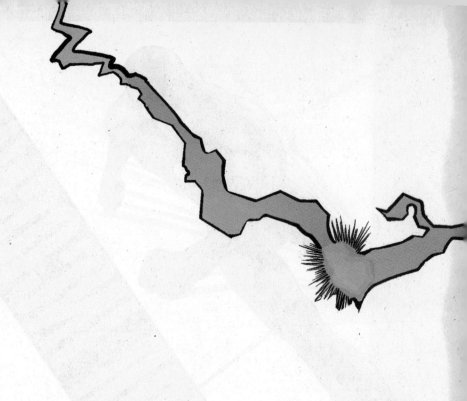
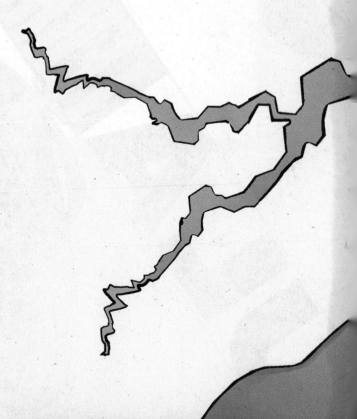

JLA TERROR INCOGNITA

Mark Waid Chuck Dixon Scott Beatty Writers Mike S. Miller Bryan Hitch Darryl Banks

Cliff Rathburn Pencillers Paul Neary Dave Meikis Wayne Faucher Inkers David Baron

Laura DePuy Colorists Ken Lopez Bill Oakley Letterers

JLA: TERROR INCOGNITA. Published by DC Comics. Cover and compilation copyright © 2002 DC Comics. All Rights Reserved. Originally published in single magazine form as JLA 55-60. Copyright © 2001, 2002 DC Comics. All Rights Reserved. All characters, their distinctive likenesses and related indicia featured in this publication are trademarks of DC Comics. The stories, characters, and incidents featured in this publication are entirely fictional. DC Comics does not read or accept unsolicited submissions of ideas, stories or artwork. DC Comics, 1700 Broadway, New York, NY 10019. A division of Warner Bros. — An AOL Time Warner Company. Printed in Canada. First Printing. ISBN: 1-56389-936-1. Cover illustration by Bryan Hitch & Paul Neary. Cover color by Laura DePuy. Publication design by Louis Prandi.

LIGHT?

SURE.

THERE'S A SERIAL KILLER LOOSE IN DENVER...

SO, YOU--

SKRICH

--YOU COME HERE--

SKRICH

--COME HERE OFTEN--?

SKRICH   SKRICH
SKRICH

HANG ON, HANG ON...

...AND DETECTIVE JOHN JONES HAS JUST SPOTTED HIS PRIME SUSPECT.

SKRICH
SKRICH

:SIGH: HEY, HANDSOME--YOU GOT A LIGHT?

HANG ON!

UNTIL NOW, JONES'S QUARRY HAS BEEN ELUSIVE, ALMOST EPHEMERAL--

--A PHANTOM EVAPORATING IN THE SPOTLIGHT OF INVESTIGATION.

FOR A MOMENT, JONES--A.K.A. J'ONN J'ONZZ OF THE JLA--WONDERS IF THE SUSPECT SECRETLY WANTS TO BE CAUGHT. THAT'S A PSYCHOLOGICAL TRAIL J'ONZZ HAS BEEN DOWN MORE THAN ONCE...

...BUT IT HAS NEVER LED HERE.

H'RONMEER...!

CAME THE PALE RIDERS

MARK WAID   BRYAN HITCH   PAUL NEARY
STORY   PENCILS   INKS

LAURA DEPUY   KEN LOPEZ   STEVE WACKER   DAD RASPLER
COLORS   LETTERS   ASSISTANT EDITOR   EDITOR

WHO, ME? WELL, IF YOU'RE OFFERING...

UMM... HONEY...

YOU TWO KNOW *BETTER* THAN *THIS!* LEAVE YOUR LOVE LIFE *OUTSIDE* THESE DOORS!

I *DISAGREE,* PERRY! EVERYBODY KNOWS WHAT BELONGS IN THE *NEWSROOM--*

OLSEN! HAVE YOU SEEN LANE'S *PROFESSIONALISM* AROUND HERE SOMEWHERE? IT SEEMS TO BE *MISSING!*

THIS SORT OF THING HAS *NO PLACE* IN HERE!

--IS *NEWS!*

PERRY EDITOR

12

NICE CATCH. SHE'S THE ONE, RIGHT?

LATEST IN A GROWING LINE OF FORTUNE TELLERS AND "PSYCHICS" REPORTEDLY STALKED BY ECTOPLASMIC ENTITIES.

IT'S OKAY TO USE THE WORD "GHOSTS," YOU KNOW.

IF I BELIEVED IN THEM, NIGHTWING, I SUPPOSE I COULD.

FUNNY. LET'S PLAY WORD ASSOCIATION. THE SPECTRE. SAMSARA.

DEADMA--

DEAD.

MAN.

SKNKPT

YES? YOU WERE SAYING?

14

MURMANSK.

A NAVAL PORT POPULATED BY A HALF-MILLION RUSSIANS.

EVEN UNDER OPTIMUM CONDITIONS, HEAT AND NOURISHMENT ARE RARE COMMODITIES IN MURMANSK.

THESE ARE HARDLY OPTIMUM CONDITIONS.

FOR SIX DAYS, THE CITY HAS BEEN SUFFERING FROM A TOTAL POWER BLACKOUT. STILL, WORD OF ARRIVING SUPPLIES HAS SPREAD--

--WHIPPING THE STARVING POPULACE INTO A BATTLE FOR FOOD--

--THAT NOT EVERYONE IS STRONG ENOUGH TO FIGHT--

--WITHOUT HELP.

‹WHAT'S YOUR NAME, LITTLE ONE?›

BY THE WAY, PRINCESS, NOT TO PLAY FASHION POLICE OR ANYTHING, BUT THIS GROUP SEEMS PERILOUSLY SHORT OF TIARAS.

IXNAY ON THE OKESJAY. SOME POLI-SCI UPSET ON PARADISE ISLAND. NO MORE "PRINCESS." AQUAMAN WARNED ME ABOUT IT JUST BEFORE HE CUT OUT ON PERSONAL BUSINESS.

I MEAN... I...LIKE WHAT YOU'VE DONE WITH... YOUR HAIR...

YEAH. SMOOTH.

SO HERE'S A FUN FACT. DID YOU KNOW WE'RE STANDING IN ONE OF THE MOST DANGEROUS CITIES ON EARTH?

YOU'RE KIDDING.

HE'S NOT. THAT THING ON CABLE, RIGHT?

A TRAVELOGUE. TURNS OUT MURMANSK BOASTS UNUSUALLY HIGH NUMBERS OF BOTH DECOMMISSIONED NUCLEAR SUBS AND SHUT-DOWN NUCLEAR POWER PLAN--

<STOP THEM YOU MUST STOP THEM!>

WHOA! SLOW DOWN! PRIN-ER--

--DIANA-- CAN YOU TRANSLATE?

HE'S SAYING--

--MERCIFUL GAEA--

--A SMALL GROUP OF ENGINEERS STRIPPED FUEL FROM A SUBMARINE--

--SO THEY CAN REVIVE A POWER STATION--?

YOU'RE KIDDING! THOSE DUMPS ARE DEATHTRAPS EVEN WITHOUT NUCLEAR FODDER!

I KNOW THESE PEOPLE ARE DESPERATE, BUT THIS COULD--

OH, GOD.

PHOENIX, ARIZONA.

OVER THE PAST TWO WEEKS, POSTAL CARRIER JERRY HALLORAN HAS COME TO *LOATHE* THIS PART OF HIS ROUTE.

THIS PARTICULAR *OFFICE BUILDING* RARELY, IF EVER, RECEIVES ANYTHING NOT MARKED "OCCUPANT." THERE'S NOTHING AT ALL EVEN *REMOTELY* REMARKABLE ABOUT IT.

SO WHY IS IT, JERRY WONDERS, THAT A FAINT *NAUSEA* OVERWHELMS HIM WHENEVER HE WALKS BY.

A SIGHT? A SMELL? HE CAN'T FIGURE IT OUT. ALL HE'S SURE OF IS THAT THE LONGER HE *DAWDLES*--

--THE WORSE IT *GETS.* SOMETHING ABOUT THE PLACE-- SOMETHING--

--PUSHES HIM GENTLY *AWAY*--

--LEAVING HIM *CONVINCED* THAT WHATEVER IS INSIDE--

--HE WOULD NEVER WANT TO SEE.

HELLO, J'ONN.

DON'T MIND THE DECOR.

MURMANSK, RUSSIA.

THE ONLY THING STANDING BETWEEN THE LOCAL POPULATION AND ENOUGH LINGERING RADIATION TO MELT A GEIGER COUNTER IS A RING-CONSTRUCTED DOME CONJURED BY GREEN LANTERN.

THANKS TO HIM, FLASH, PLASTIC MAN AND WONDER WOMAN, A HALF-MILLION INNOCENTS WERE JUST SPARED THE IMPACT OF A NUCLEAR BLAST.

THEY'RE NOT PARTICULARLY GRATEFUL.

KEEP OW OW OW KEEP BLOCKING OW OW OW OW--

--BLOCKING FOR LANTERN OWWW!

HE GOES DOWN, WE ARE POPCORN IN A MICROWAVE!

THEY'RE UNARMED, BUT THAT'S NOT STOPPING THEM! TRY NOT TO LET THEM HURT THEMSELVES!

GOOD LUCK! THEY CAN'T BE REASONED WITH! MIND CONTROL?

POSSIBLY-- BUT IF SOMEONE'S GOING TO THE TROUBLE OF MANIPULATING OTHERS TO STRIKE AT US--

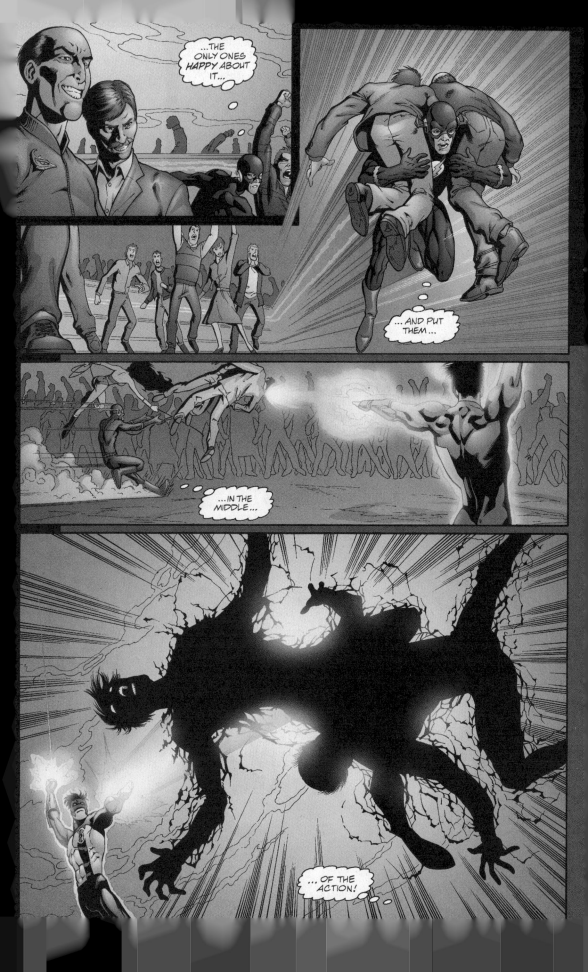

NOT *YOU.* I'VE BEEN FOLLOWING A RECENT RASH OF *ODD ABDUCTIONS* AROUND THE GLOBE. SELF-STYLED *MYSTICS* AND *FORTUNE-TELLERS*... LEGENDARY *GAMBLERS,* TOP *DETECTIVES*...

...MOST OF WHOM, WITNESSES SAY, CLAIMED THEY WERE BEING *"HAUNTED"* JUST BEFORE THEY *VANISHED.* NO OTHER *CONNECTION.*

BUT IF I PLOT THEIR LAST KNOWN *WHEREABOUTS* AGAINST THOSE OF THE BRAIN-WASHED *MARTIANS*... ADD IN WHAT FEW, ABORTED TRAILS THE AUTHORITIES *HAVE* FOUND...

...IT SUGGESTS THE MARTIANS ARE CONGREGATING IN DOWNTOWN. *PHOENIX, ARIZONA*... GATHERING *VICTIMS* ALONG THE WAY.

COINCIDENCE? THEY COULDN'T *POSSIBLY* BE *CONNECTED*...

WHICH, LEAGUE HISTORY *TELLS* US, GENERALLY MEANS THEY *ARE* SOMEHOW.

I'M *TELEPORTING* TO *PHOENIX* AND HOPING I FIND J'ONN STILL *ALIVE* THERE.

J'ONN? WHAT DO YOU MEAN, *"STILL ALIVE"?*

HE'S *ALSO* AMONG THE MISSING-- AND HE'D BE THE FIRST ONE THEY'D GO AFTER. I'LL *CALL* IF I NEED *BACKUP.*

FORGIVE ME...I KNOW YOU'RE *BATMAN* AND ALL...BUT HOW DO YOU *SNEAK* PAST TELEPATHS?

LET *ME* WORRY ABOUT THAT.

NEURAL AMPLIFIER OF BRAINWAVE

--AND THAT'S THE LAST OF THE MURMANSKIANS. I'VE RINGED THEM FREE AND CLEAR.

SUPERMAN? WHAT NOW?

TRY IT. LIGHT A FIRE.

NOTHING. WHY, PLEASE?

SKRIT SKRIT SKRIT

THE GOOD NEWS IS, AT LEAST WE KNOW THE ENEMY... AND, LIKE J'ONN, THEY'RE VULNERABLE TO FLAME.

WE ALL LIGHT OUR ZIPPOS, WE CAN'T BE TOUCHED. THERE IS, AT LEAST, THAT.

TRY IT.

BECAUSE THE MARTIANS HAVE BEEN BUSY. SOMEHOW, THEY'VE FOUND A WAY TO INTRODUCE A GROWING NUMBER OF VIRAL SUBATOMIC PARTICLES INTO THE ATMOSPHERE.

PARTICLES THAT ATTACH TO OXYGEN ATOMS TO SLOW COMBUSTION.

THAT SOUNDS BAD.

IT IS.

IT'S ALREADY *CRIPPLED YOUR* AREA AND IT'S *SPREADING WORLDWIDE.* RIGHT NOW, WITHIN A *HUNDRED* MILES OF PITTSBURGH, ALL *COMBUSTION* ENGINES HAVE *FAILED.*

I'VE GOT *FIRESTORM* DOING HIS BEST TO *TRANSMUTE* THE PARTICLES AWAY, BUT--

--BUT I BARELY *KNOW* WHAT I'M *WORKING* WITH! THIS WAS *NEVER* ON THE *CHEMISTRY FINALS--* AND THERE'S *SO MUCH--!*

"--HE'S ON HIS OWN."

BATMAN, CAN YOU GET A LEAD ON THE *HOW* AND THE *WHERE* OF THIS? BATMAN?

HE'S DROPPED CONTACT, SUPERMAN. UNTIL FURTHER NOTICE--

THERE'S SUCH A THING AS HIDING *TOO WELL. EVERY* OFFICE BUILDING THIS SIZE HIRES *JANITORIAL SERVICES,* RECEIVES *DELIVERIES,* HAS *SOME* FOOT TRAFFIC.

BUT NOT *THIS* ONE. WHY? WHAT DON'T THE MARTIANS WANT US TO SEE...?

EYAAAAH!

FWNSSHH!

PROXIMITY RANGE BREACHED

DEET

‹J'ONZZ...!
HE'S
GONE!›

‹WE TURNED
OUR BACKS
FOR ONLY A
SECOND! WHERE
COULD HE
HAVE--›

GHYAAARGHHH!

J'ONN...? HOW...HOW
LONG HAVE THEY HAD
YOU? HOW LONG HAVE
THEY BEEN
OPERATIVE?

WHO
REVIVED
THEM?

H'RONMEER
FORGIVE ME... ...I DID.

45

--HARD TO IMAGINE **WORSE**, CLARK. **ALL-OUT** WAR AGAINST AN ARMY OF **INVISIBLE TELEPATHS**.

ANY THOUGHTS OF **STRATEGY?**

NOT YET. IN THE MEANTIME, LET'S TALK **EARTH SCIENCE**.

WHAT THE MARTIANS HAVE *INTRODUCED* IS AN ALIEN ION THAT SUPPRESSES THE *ELECTRON FLOW OF CHEMICAL REACTIONS.*

BAD *ENOUGH* MATTER WON'T COM-*BUST.* PLANT LIFE'S BEGUN TO ASPHYXIATE AND DIE. IF WE DON'T *STOP* THIS, WE CAN COUNT THE *HOURS* TO *HUMAN EXTINCTION.*

WHICH MEANS FINDING THE STATIONS *PRODUCING* THE IONS-- AND *THAT,* I CAN DO.

THE THICKER THE IONS HANG IN THE *AIR,* THE CLOSER I AM TO THEIR *SOURCE.*

HEY! DON'T HOG *ALL* THE FUN!

MURMANSK?

CALMER-- SO WE FOLLOWED YOUR *SIGNAL DEVICE.* YOU'RE ABSOLUTELY SURE *YOU* CAN TRACK DOWN *ALL* THE ION STATIONS?

NOW THAT I KNOW WHAT I'M *LOOKING* FOR. THEY'RE COMING *DOWN--* BEGINNING WITH *THIS* ONE.

WITHIN *DAYS*, PERHAPS *HOURS*, THE HUMAN RACE WILL BE *EXTINCT* UNLESS THE *JUSTICE LEAGUE* MANAGES TO TURN THE TIDE OF *BATTLE*...

WHAT IN THE--?

SHKOOM

...*AGAINST* AN *ENEMY* WHO CAN DO *THIS*.

MINDOVERMATTER

MARK WAID·STORY

MIKE S. MILLER·PENCILS

PAUL NEARY·INKS

DAVID BARON·COLORS

KEN LOPEZ·LETTERS

STEVE WACKER·ASSISTANT EDITOR

DAN RASPLER·EDITOR

"--YOU CAN'T TRUST ANYTHING YOU SEE!"

AND NOW, TO ILLUSTRATE MY POINT...

...OH, THIS IS SO VERY BAD...

PLAS! PLAS, IT'S ME--!

DON'T LISTEN TO HIM! HE'S LYING! I'M OVER HERE!

NO, PLAS! DON'T FALL FOR IT!

THEY'RE LYING!

EENIE, MEENIE, MINEY, D'OH...

I KNOW THIS ONE! I KNOW THIS ONE! ONE'S REAL BUT OHGOD OHGOD, THE OTHER THREE ARE MARTIANS...

...I DON'T WANNA PLAY THIS GAME...

A LITTLE ♪ HELP, ♫ KY-YULL...!

OKAY...

...O'BRIANNNN...!

OH, YEAH! THAT'S THE STUFF!

WHO KNOWS MY REAL NAME? ONLY THE BONA FIDE, BABY!

OR A TELEPATH.

EYAAAAAAAH!

SHZZZZAK!

LOOK AT HIM CRAWL. PATHETIC.

MELT HIM.

DIANA... HUH-HELP... ME...

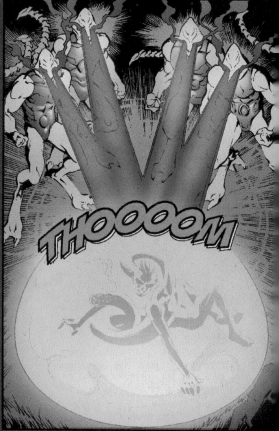

THOOOOM

GET AWAY FROM HIM.

"IT'S GETTING WORSE, CLARK. ZATANNA'S FIGHTING TO KEEP A WARD OF PREMATURE INFANTS BREATHING...

"...BUT SHE SAYS THE MARTIANS HAVE TARGETED THE MAGIC USERS. THERE'S A 'PSYCHIC BLANKET' PREVENTING THEM FROM USING THEIR SPELLS."

BUT I'VE GOTTEN A FIX ON THE TOWERS-- ONE ON EVERY CONTINENT! THOSE HAVE TO BE OUR FIRST PRIORITY!

BREAK OFF THE FIGHT-- NOW!

HOW? WE ARE SO OUT GUNN--

AAAAAGH!

SNAP

FIND A WAY! SIX BILLION PEOPLE ARE ABOUT TO DRAW THEIR FINAL BREATH! FIND A--

--WAIT--!

TOWER NEUTRALIZED

TOWER NEUTRALIZED TOWER NEUTRALIZED TOWER NEUTRALIZED

"DISREGARD. STAND YOUR GROUND AND KNOW THAT HELP--"

J'ONN...? IS... THAT REALLY... YOU?

I'M SORRY, KYLE.

SUPERMAN...

...THIS WAY.

INCOMING.

CAN WE *TAKE* THEM?

THEY'LL ONLY SEND *MORE*--AND *MORE AGAIN*. THEY CAN SEE US, *FIND* US FROM *ANYWHERE* ON EARTH.

BUT UNTIL THEY REALIZE I'M *AMONG* YOU-- AND THAT WON'T TAKE *LONG*--

KRAK

--I CAN MAKE THEM SEE WHAT I *WANT* THEM TO SEE.

SUPERMAN, I LEFT *FLASH* BESIDE A SURPRISED AND UNCONSCIOUS MARTIAN FORTY MILES *EAST*.

RETRIEVE HIM, BUT TAKE *CARE*. BY NOW, HIS METABOLISM WILL HAVE HEALED ONLY HIS MOST *SEVERE* INJURIES. AND BRING *BATMAN*.

"--BUT ONCE HE'S LOST THE ELEMENT OF SURPRISE--"

≈FWEEET!≈

THOOM

--THE REST IS UP TO US.

GOOD BOY.

KNOW THIS: THE FORTRESS ARSENAL CONTAINS WEAPONS I'VE CONFISCATED FROM DOZENS OF GALACTIC DESPOTS AND WARMONGERS THIS--

--IS THE *LEAST* OF THEM.

PHASE-SHIFT.

DEPLOY AS MANY ARMAMENTS AS YOU *LIKE*, "SUPERMAN." IT SEEMS THEY'RE EFFECTIVE ONLY AGAINST *SOLID* TARGETS. MARTIAN MOLECULES...

...HAVE AN *ATOMIC RESONANCE* NO MATTER *HOW* IMMATERIAL THEY BECOME... ...CREEP.

GYAAHEE!!

NNNNUHHHHH!

KRAUNCH

YIPPR—

KRYPTO!

THAT'S IT...JUST A FEW MORE SECONDS...

...WATCHING HELPLESSLY IN A *WRAITHLIKE* STATE AS WE SYSTEMATICALLY *REBUILD* OUR TOWERS AND... *CLEANSE* THE EARTH...

...TAKING *PARTICULAR* NOTE, I MIGHT ADD, *SPECIFICALLY* OF YOUR FRIENDS AND *LOVED* ONES...

...NONE OF YOU ABLE TO LIFT A *PHANTOM* FINGER TO PROTECT THEM WHILE WE SAVOR YOUR *ANGUISH* AND *FRUSTRATION*...

...THAT'S SIMPLY TOO GOOD AN OPPORTUNITY TO LET *PASS*.

WHAT HAVE YOU TO SAY TO *THAT*...?

VICTORY IS THEIRS.

--BUT GIVEN THEIR SPEED AND THEIR STEALTH--

THE WHITE MARTIANS RUN RAMPANT OVER THE FACE OF THE EARTH. THANKS TO THE JLA, THEY ARE ONCE MORE VUL-NERABLE TO THEIR ONE WEAKNESS--OPEN FLAME--

--THAT'S NOT MUCH OF A THREAT.

IN AN *ALARMINGLY* BRIEF TIME, THE MARTIANS HAVE MANAGED TO NEUTRALIZE ANY OPPOSITION THAT MIGHT *ARISE*--

--BECAUSE EARTH'S *PRIMARY CHAMPIONS*--THE LEGENDARY HEROES OF THE *JUSTICE LEAGUE*--

DYING BREATH

MARK WAID
STORY

MIKE MILLER
PENCILS

PAUL NEARY
INKS

DAVID BARON
COLORS

KEN LOPEZ
LETTERS

STEVE WACKER
ASSISTANT ED.

DAN RASPLER
EDITOR

IF THEY THREW US IN HERE TO **TORTURE** US, IT'S **WORKING.** RING US **OUT** OF HERE, MAN!

PLEASE. IT'S LIKE TRYING TO PICK A LOCK WITH A **WET NOODLE.** YOU **HAVE NOTICED** WE'RE NOT EXACTLY IN THE LAND OF **NEWTON-IAN PHYSICS,** RIGHT? WE'RE **HERE--**

--BECAUSE I **BROUGHT** US HERE.

YOU **WHAT?**

PROTEX HAD US COMPLETELY AT HIS **MERCY.** PUNISHING US BY MAKING US **WATCH** THE MARTIAN INVASION INSTEAD OF SIMPLY MURDERING US **OUTRIGHT--**

--HE'S NOT THAT **FOOLISH.** BUT BY **BAITING** HIM WITH AN **AWARENESS** OF THE ZONE, THEN MENTALLY... "**ENCOURAGING**" OUR **BANISHMENT--**

--I DELIBERATELY **ARRANGED** FOR US TO BE SENT **HERE--**

--TO THE **ONE PLACE** WHERE AN ARMY OF **TELEPATHS** CANNOT "**HEAR**" OUR PLANS.

WELL **DONE.**

'KAY, BUT EVEN IF WE WRITE A WHOLE **PLAYBOOK,** HOW DO WE GET BACK **HOME?** HUH? HUH?

ARRANGEMENTS HAVE BEEN **MADE.** AS **BATMAN** WELL KNOWS, WE'VE BEEN EMPLOYING A..."**SECRET WEAPON**" FOR **SOME TIME.**

MOREOVER, I HAVE ARRIVED AT WHAT MIGHT BE OUR **ONLY HOPE...**

"... SO LISTEN CLOSELY."

UNACCEPTABLE. JONN, YOU'VE JUST OUTLINED YOUR OWN *SUICIDE!*

NO. MY *REDEMPTION.* THE MARTIANS *AWOKE* BECAUSE OF *MY* MISTAKE.

UNLIKELY.

WHAT... WHAT WERE WE JUST *TALKING* ABOUT?

WELL, (A) THAT DOESN'T MEAN WE'RE GONNA LET YOU DO *THIS...*

...AND (B) EVEN IF WE *DID* DECIDE YOUR PLAN WAS WORKABLE, WE'RE BACK WHERE WE *STARTED.* YOU SAID *YOURSELF* YOU DON'T HAVE ENOUGH POWER TO SHIELD YOUR THOUGHTS *AND* OURS!

THEY'LL READ THIS STRATEGY OFF OUR BRAINS LIKE THEY WERE *BILLBOARDS!*

YOU'LL *REMEMBER.* YOU'LL *EACH* REMEMBER YOUR ROLE WHEN THE RIGHT MOMENT *COMES...*

...AND IT'S *TOO LATE* TO *STOP* ME.

77

EARTHLINGS. WHAT AN EMBARRASSINGLY *LOW* TOLERANCE FOR PAIN THEY HAVE.

Z'USH, TELL TEAM DEIMOS TO RESUME CONSTRUCTION ON THE *FLAME DAMPING TOWERS.* TEAM PHOBOS IS TO CONTINUE THE *PLANETARY CLEANSING* UNTIL THE HUMANS ARE COMPLETELY--

ZEE ZEE ZEE ZEE

AAAH! WHAT IS THAT *SOUND?*

ADJUSTING AURAL SENSORS TO *ACCOMMODATE...*

GOT YOUR ATTENTION? GOOD.

THIS IS THE *JUSTICE LEAGUE.* WE'RE NARROWCASTING ON AN ULTRAFREQUENCY ONLY YOU AND YOUR PEOPLE CAN *HEAR,* PROTEX.

THE RED ONES--THEY'RE FLEEING!

PROVING THAT HUMANS ARE, AT HEART, COWARDS.

LET THEM RUN, Z'USH. THERE IS NOWHERE THEY CAN HIDE WHERE WE CANNOT FIND THEM.

BESIDES, THEY ARE THE LEAST OF OUR ENEMIES. ONCE THESE FOUR ARE VANQUISHED--

COMMANDER--?

AN OPTICAL ABERRATION. J'ONZZ ATTEMPTING TO WORM THROUGH MY MINDSHIELDS, PERHAPS--

"-- AND FAILING."

YOUR PERDURABLE COMPASSION FOR THE CARBON CATTLE WHO DRAG THEIR HEELS ACROSS YOUR PLANET NEVER CEASES TO AMAZE ME.

DO YOU THINK US BOLDLY ELATED THAT YOU CHOSE THIS AS YOUR BATTLEFIELD? A FLAMELESS VACUUM?

HARDLY.

AIRLESSNESS CHEATS US OF THE MUSIC--

-OF THE SOUND I HAVE BEEN LONGING TO HEAR:

"SNAP."

AAAAAAGHH!

"YES. WHICH IS
WHY WE...REQUIRED
AN AGENT...

"...WHO COULD
WORK FROM THE
INSIDE."

OUR FAILING POWERS CANNOT PROTECT ANY OF US, PROTEX! LET ME *SAVE* YOU WHILE I STILL *CAN!*

SUBMIT--OR DIE WITH ME! WHICH WILL IT BE?

AHH, NO! FIRESTORM AND CAPTAIN ATOM TO SAN ANDREAS STAT!

EIGHT SECONDS LEFT TO REVERSE TRAJECTORY! SEVEN!

J'ONN! EARTH IS BREAKING! WE'RE OUT OF TIME!

SUBMIT OR DIE! SUBMIT OR--

WE SUBMIT!

WE SUBMIT...!

OH, GOD...

IS-- IS HE--

HANG ON!

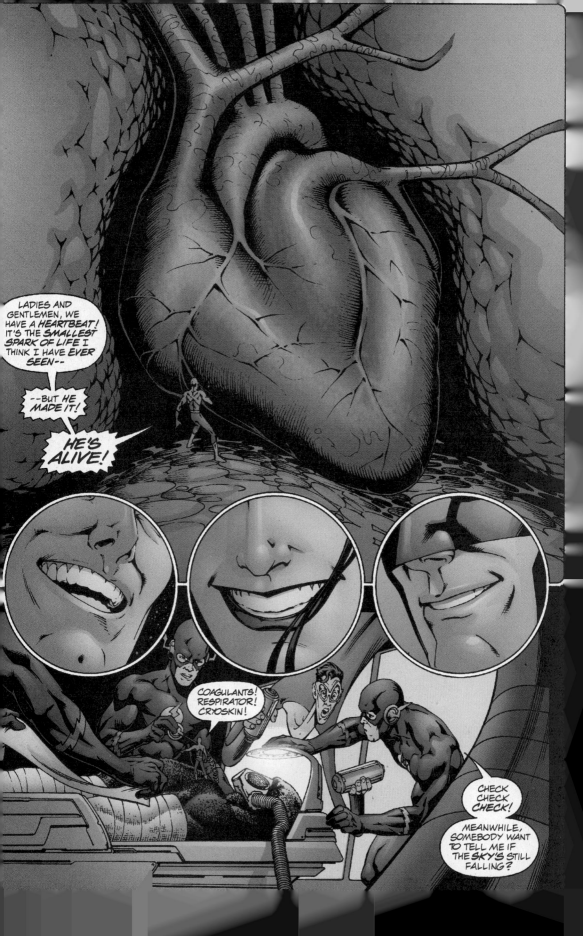

THE ELLSWORTH MOUNTAINS, ANTARCTICA.

WE SHOULD BE GETTING *CLOSE,* KATHERINE.

I'LL TAKE A POSITION READING.

ACCORDING TO THE *G.P.S.* RIG, WE'RE NEARING THE *SOUTH POLE.*

THAT'S *GREAT!* AHEAD OF SCHEDULE.

YOU DON'T UNDERSTAND, KEITH. WE'RE *NEARING* IT EVEN AS WE *STAND* HERE.

WHAT ARE YOU *SAYING,* KATH?

IT'S LIKE THE POLE WAS COMING TOWARD *US.*

DEATH VALLEY, CALIFORNIA.

TEMPORARY META-VILLAIN DETENTION CAMP.

"LOOKS LIKE YOU'RE A FEW CARDS *SHORT*, SUPERMAN."

NOT EVEN A *STRAIGHT*, UNLESS YOU COUNT THESE BUMS AS THREE KNAVES.

DANGER! LETHAL VOLTAGE
ESCAPEES WILL BE SHOT ON SIGHT!

BIG BOSS

JACK AND QUEEN DIDN'T MAKE IT, GENERAL TANNER.

WE'RE LEARNING THE HARD WAY THAT BEING "JOKERIZED" IS EITHER PERMANENT OR *FATAL*.

AFTER A CERTAIN DURATION, THE ANTISERUM DOESN'T *WORK*.

I TRUST YOU'RE *SEGREGATING* THE ONES WHO ARE STILL AFFLICTED?

NORMALS IN THE NORTH QUAD, LOONIES TO THE SOUTH... AND JACKALS COMIN' IN STRONG FROM THE EAST.

LAWYERS GOT BETTER HUMVEES THAN WE DO!

AND YOU'VE HAD NO *DISCIPLINARY* PROBLEMS?

NONE *SO* FAR. IT'S LIKE *MOST* OF 'EM HAVE WHOPPER HANGOVERS FROM THE JOKER-JUICE.

THE LOONIER ONES ARE PLANNING SOME KINDA *VARIETY* SHOW FOR THEIR FELLOW DETAINEES.

UH... SUPERMAN...

--TELL ME THAT'S NOT ANOTHER ROUND OF JOKER'S "CRAZY RAIN."

IT'S *NOT.*

IT'S THE *AURORA AUSTRALIS.*

TELL HIM WHAT YOU'RE SCANNING, SUPERMAN.

GREAT KRYPTON...

WHAT *IS* IT? WHAT DO YOU *SEE?*

A *MAGNETIC STORM.*

A THOUSAND LEY LINES INTER-SECTING WHERE THEY *SHOULDN'T.*

IT'S *DOCTOR POLARIS*, ISN'T IT?

HE'S DISRUPTING THE SOUTH POLE... POSSIBLY *ABSORBING* IT. J'ONN'S ALREADY NOTED SIGNIFICANT CLIMATIC CHANGES.

I SUGGEST YOU *MEET* US EN ROUTE.

AND *DON'T* USE THE TELEPORTERS.

THE MAGNETIC FIELD IS DISRUPTING THE TRANSIT BEAMS... AND WE'VE ALREADY HAD ONE *NEAR MISS* TODAY.

WOOZY...

LAST GUY THERE GET'S THE OTHER ONE'S MONITOR DUTY FOR A MONTH.

READYSET*GO!*

WHY DOES EVERY FLASH FEEL *COMPELLED* TO RACE ME?

IT'S WHAT SPEEDSTERS *DO!*

"FASTEST MAN ALIVE" AND ALL THAT!

THE BUZZING *FOLLOWS* US WHEREVER I GO.

BUZZ
BUZZ
BUZZ
BUZZ

Shush... WE NEED TO *CONCEN-TRATE*.

I SAID YOU COULD STAY IF YOU PROMISED US YOU WOULD BE *QUIET*.

AWWK!

AWWK!

WE *CAN'T* HAVE ALL THIS BUZZING IF I'M GOING TO GET BETTER.

OUR READINGS PINPOINT THE SOUTH POLE MEANDERING TWENTY MILES NORTH NORTHEAST OF ITS *STANDARD* POSI-TION.

THAT'S POLARIS, J'ONN.

THE DOC IS BAD, *BAD* NEWS. NOW HE'S JOKERFIED AND IN CONTROL OF THE WORLD'S ELECTROMAG-NETIC FIELD.

WE SHOULD BE ABLE TO APPROACH.

THIS SHUTTLE IS OF CERAMIC-BASED CON-STRUCTION.

WOOG!

BLAST-- YOU SPOKE TOO SOON, J'ONN! PULL OUT!

INCREDIBLE. NO RESPONSE--POLARIS MUST BE CONTROLLING THE SHUTTLE.

THERE MUST BE MICRO-METALLOID ELEMENTS IN THE CERAMICS.

BLOW THE *HATCH!* I'LL *CUSHION* US WITH MY RING!

NOT SURE THERE IS-- --*TIME* FOR THAT!

WHOOM!

HA! AND THERE THEY GO! WELL, WHAT CAN I SAY?

BUZZ! BUZZ! BUZZ!

YOWTCH!

FWOO-SHOOM!

OW!

UH!

OOCH!

:gasp:

NEXT TIME CHECK ME THROUGH **BAGGAGE,** GANG.

OH.

SO I THINK WE CAN AGREE THAT **I** WON?

WE'LL DISCUSS THIS **LATER,** WALLY.

IT'S DEFINITELY **POLARIS.**

THAT GUY'S **SERIOUS** TROUBLE.

WORSE THAN THAT, HE'S AT THE **NEXUS** OF THE SOUTHERN HEMISPHERE'S MAGNETIC FIELD.

EXACTLY. RIGHT NOW, HE **IS** THE SOUTH POLE.

LOOK, WE HAVE AN ENTIRE **ARMY** OF JOKERIZED META-CLOWNS TO ROUND UP.

AND IF **JOKER'S** SENT THEM ALL OVER THE **PLANET** TO RAISE HELL...

YOU KNOW THE MIND OF THE **JOKER**, BATMAN. I'LL GIVE YOU THE **NOD** ON THAT ONE.

BUT POLARIS **ISN'T** THE JOKER. I **KNOW** HIM. I'VE **FOUGHT** HIM.

THAT MAKES **ME** THE RESIDENT EXPERT HERE.

YOU CAN'T **RUSH** INTO THIS, GREEN LANTERN.

TO BEAT A **JOKER** YOU HAVE TO PLAN **AHEAD.**

POLARIS WAS INSANE **BEFORE** BEING EXPOSED TO THE JOKER-IZING TOXIN AT THE SLAB.

BUT HIS MADNESS TOOK THE FORM OF SPLIT-PERSONAL-ITIES DIVIDED FURTHER BY OBSESSIVE-COMPULSION.

IN HIS CURRENT STATE HE'S GOING TO BE EVEN MORE **CHAOTIC** THAN THAT.

I CREDITED YOU WITH MORE **SENSE** THAN TO SIMPLY RELY ON **POWER,** KYLE.

YOU HAVE TO FACTOR IN POLARIS'S STATE OF **MIND.**

AND **YOU** SHOULD KNOW WHEN TO ADMIT YOU'RE OUT OF YOUR DEPTH. THIS TIME IT **IS** ABOUT FORCE.

PUT THE EGOS **ASIDE** FOR A SECOND AND LET'S WORK THIS OUT, **OKAY?**

WE DO THIS **MY** WAY.

KNOCK YOURSELF OUT.

WHOA GUYS... WE'RE ON THE SAME **SIDE,** RIGHT?

THE BLACK HATS ARE THE ONES WITH THE PORCELAIN SKINS AND GIGGLE-FITS.

HEY! **I** HAD THE CONCH HERE!

AND I THINK **WE'RE** WINNING.

"DID YOU KNOW THAT BATMAN HAS **TASER-**CIRCUITS WIRED THROUGHOUT HIS SILLY SUIT?

"OR THAT WONDER WOMAN HAS A LOW TOLERANCE FOR HIGH-VOLTAGE ELECTROSHOCK THERAPY?

"OR THAT MARTIAN BLOOD IS NATURALLY MUCH RICHER IN **IRON** THAN HUMAN HEMOGLOBIN?

"AND YOU, YOUNG GREEN LANTERN, WHY **DO** YOU KEEP HITTING YOURSELF WITH YOUR SHINY LITTLE RING?"

WE TRIED IT *YOUR* WAY, KYLE.

LET'S GET THE "I-TOLD-YOU-SO'S" OVER WITH, OKAY?

HOW *FAR* ARE WE FROM POLARIS?

I GUESSTIMATE HIS RANGE AT A HUNDRED MILES.

THAT'S IN EVERY DIRECTION, *INCLUDING* UP AND DOWN.

THE LADY'S *RIGHT.*

HE HAS A *COUNTER* FOR EVERY ONE OF US.

SO HOW DO WE ISOLATE OR DEFEAT HIM?

THERE'S AT LEAST A *TRACE* OF METAL IN ALL OF US.

NOT *ALL* OF US.

WUDZ EDDYDUDDY OOKING AD?

DON'D I GED DUH FODE?

READY, KYLE?

AS I'M GONNA BE.

ALL HOPE RESTS WITH YOU, MR. O'BRIAN!

DANKZ ZO MUSH.

guh!

WHAT'S THIS?

GID UG GEVORE ZUMBUDDY GEDS HURD.

HA HA HA HA HA!

YOU'RE THEIR PLAN?

WHICHEVER SUPER-CRETIN THREW YOU AT US MISSED!

DON'T HOLD BACK-- GIVE IT EVERYTHING YOU'VE GOT!

GET IT RIGHT OR PLASTIC MAN FRIES.

HE DID VOLUNTEER FOR THIS, RIGHT?

CUT THE CHATTER. POLARIS IS CRAZY... NOT STUPID.

WE'VE ONLY GOT ONE SHOT AT THIS BEFORE HE FIGURES US OUT.

"SUPERMAN HITS THE AURORA AUSTRALIS WITH A CONCENTRATED BEAM OF HEAT-VISION.

"IT BANKS EARTHWARD AND THEN IT'S *YOUR* TURN, KYLE."

NOD DAD FUDDY, BOLAZIZ.

HA HA HA HA HA HA

huh?

ahhh...

THAT MAKES ME--

--TOASTY!

GAAAAH!

ONE NASTY, PSYCHOTIC LIVING LODESTONE SEALED IN HIS *OWN* NUMMY JUICES!

YOW! YAK!

"*NOW* WHAT DO WE DO WITH HIM?"

DRAINING POLARIS OF THE EXCESS ELECTROMAGNETIC ENERGY WON'T BE EASY... AND THAT'S *ASSUMING* THE ANTI-SERUM REVERSES HIS JOKERIZATION.

THEN LEAVE HIM WHERE HE IS.

J'ONN CAN HOLD HIM WITH PSYCHIC BAFFLES UNTIL WE CLEAN UP THE *REST* OF THE MESS.

PLASTIC MAN STAYS JUST IN CASE.

I SUGGEST YOU BUILD THEM BOTH A SHELTER AND REPLENISH YOUR STRENGTH.

THE HOLE IN THE OZONE LAYER SHOULD *HASTEN* YOUR SOLAR RECHARGE.

WHAT ABOUT *YOU?*

I'M HEADED BACK TO GOTHAM TO PUT AN END TO THIS.

LOOK, BATMAN... I'M SORRY I DOUBTED YOU. YOU *DO* HAVE MORE EXPERIENCE AT THIS THAN THE REST OF US.

I COULD *FLY* YOU...

GOTHAM'S *MY* CONCERN.

JUST DEAL WITH THE REMAINING JOKER-IZED METAS

AND REMEMBER TO *PLAN* AHEAD, KYLE.

"*ALWAYS* PLAN AHEAD."

JLA

AND NEXT MONTH: "MERRY CHRISTMAS JLA... HOPE YOU SURVIVE IT!"

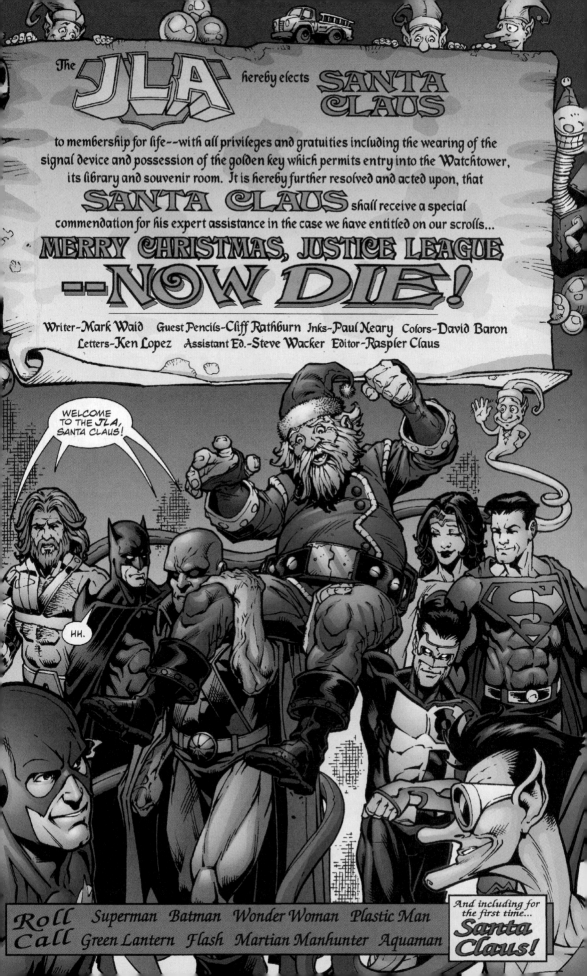

"IT WAS *JUST LAST NIGHT*... THE NIGHT BEFORE CHRISTMAS EVE, RIGHT? AND BIG BLUE WAS CHAIRING A *SPECIAL* MEETING TO ELECT A NEW MEMBER TO THE JLA..."

THIS "*JACOBIAN*" SEEMS TO BE MAKING QUITE A NAME FOR HIMSELF IN *GOTHAM*.

WHAT ABOUT *CHASE*? I HEAR SHE'S DOING SOME FINE WORK!

IN THE SPIRIT OF THE *SEASON*, I FIND MYSELF COMPELLED TO NOMINATE *SANTA CLAUS* FOR HIS GOOD WORKS.

"...AND THIRTY EXCRUCIATING MINUTES LATER..."

I'M SOLD! I MOVE THAT SANTA BE INDUCTED INTO THE *JUSTICE LEAGUE*!

I SECOND THE MOTION!

AND THE *EASTER BUNNY* WEPT IN SHAME.

THAT'S IT? THAT'S YOUR *BIG* STORY?

NUH... NO! NO! 'CAUSE...

...'CAUSE THEN...

"...THERE WAS A... PUFF OF... *SMOKE*..."

DENIED, JUSTICE LEAGUE! YOUR PRECIOUS *KRIS KRINGLE* IS *NO MORE*! HE IS NOW AND FOREVERMORE A *PRISONER*...

...OF HELL!

122

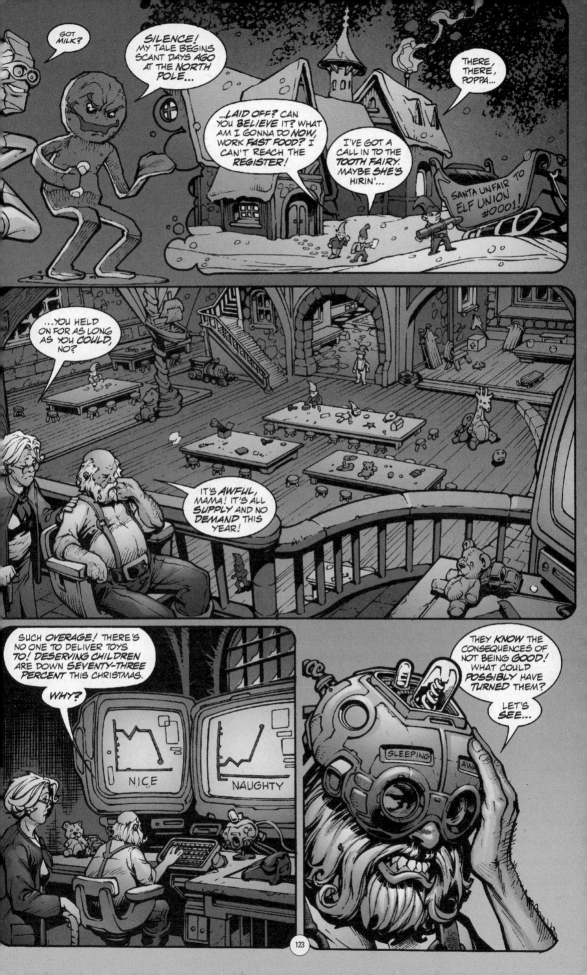

GOT MILK?

SILENCE! MY TALE BEGINS SCANT DAYS *AGO* AT THE *NORTH POLE...*

THERE, THERE, POPPA...

...*LAID OFF?* CAN YOU *BELIEVE* IT? WHAT AM I GONNA DO *NOW,* WORK *FAST FOOD?* I CAN'T REACH THE *REGISTER!*

I'VE GOT A CALL IN TO THE *TOOTH FAIRY.* MAYBE SHE'S HIRIN'...

SANTA UNFAIR TO ELF UNION #0001!

...YOU HELD ON FOR AS LONG AS YOU *COULD,* NO?

IT'S *AWFUL,* MAMA! IT'S ALL *SUPPLY* AND NO *DEMAND* THIS YEAR!

SUCH *OVERAGE!* THERE'S NO ONE TO DELIVER TOYS *TO! DESERVING* CHILDREN ARE DOWN *SEVENTY-THREE PERCENT* THIS CHRISTMAS.

WHY?

NICE

NAUGHTY

THEY *KNOW* THE CONSEQUENCES OF NOT BEING *GOOD!* WHAT COULD *POSSIBLY* HAVE *TURNED* THEM?

LET'S *SEE...*

SLEEPING

AWA

NERON?

THE *DEVIL*, DUDE! *MONSTER BAD!* HE'S ALL ABOUT THE *BARGAIN*--THAT'S HIS *SHTICK!*

HE WAS MAKING *DEALS!* GIVING *WICKED COOL TOYS*-- BUT ONLY IF YOU WERE WILLING TO DO SOMETHING *BAD* IN RETURN! AND SANTA--

"--SANTA WAS *TORQUED!*"

I HAVEN'T SEEN THAT DEMON SINCE MY *GOOD* FRIEND *PLASTIC MAN* PUT HIM DOWN!

SINGLE-HANDEDLY!

STAND *BACK,* NERON--

Welcome To NEW JERSEY

--IT'S TIME TO PUT A LITTLE *KRIS* INTO YOUR *KRINGLE!* WHY, I'LL--

?

WHAT'S THE *MATTER,* "SAINT NICK"?

YOU THINK YOU'RE THE ONLY ONE WITH A *WORKSHOP?*

AH HA HA

HA HA

125

WAS BATMAN THERE?

YES.

I LIKE BATMAN.

YES. WE ALL LOVE BATMAN. ANYWAY...

"...THE ELEMENT OF SURPRISE WAS NOT ON OUR SIDE! NERON KNEW HIS MESSENGER WOULD LURE US THERE--AND HE WAS WAITING FOR US!"

FINALLY-- THE JUSTICE LEAGUE!

GET THEM!

WITH WHAT? BIG DEAL! THOSE ARE TOY GUNS--

AAAARGH!

SSSSS

--FILLED WITH ACID!

"OF COURSE, NOTHING COULD HURT SUPERMAN..."

IT TICKLES!

"WASN'T THIS MAGIC? ISN'T SUPERMAN HURT BY MAGIC?"

"...EXCEPT, OF COURSE, ALL THE MAGIC."

OW! OW! OW!

"STILL, YOU SHOULDA SEEN US, WEEZ. DESPITE THE ODDS, WE HAD 'EM ON THE ROPES."

"WHAT WAS SANTA DOING?"

"I'M GETTING THERE.

"LANTERN DID HIS RING-THING TO CLEAR OUT THE WORKSHOP, WHILE WE--"

"WHAT WAS SANTA DOING?"

"I'M GETTING THERE."

"YOU WERE THERE."

"OKAY! OKAY! WE WERE KICKING IMP AND THRASHING NERON'S LITTLE HELL 'R' US, BUT THEN..."

GUYS, LOOK! THERE HE IS!

128

"...FLASH SPOTTED SANTA'S LITTLE 'HOLDING CELL.'

"AND THAT'S WHERE THINGS WENT REALLY SOUR.

SUPER SANTA ACTION FIGURE

SANTA'S MAGIC SACK INCLUDED

REINDEER!! SOLD SEPARATELY

WARNING

3+

"'CAUSE WHILE WE WERE BUSY DE-MINTING NERON'S COLLECTIBLE LITTLE TRAP--

NERON

NERON STILL

MORE FOR NERON

ME, ME, ME

"--NERON, WHO KNEW VERY WELL WHAT BELONGED IN HIS STOCKING--

OUR ONLY HOPE OF SALVATION, WEEZ, LAY IN THE GLOVED HANDS OF THE MAN. THE MAN SOME CALL PERE NOEL.

"HE WAS IN *LUCK.* WE HADN'T MANAGED TO SPRING HIM *OUTRIGHT*-- BUT WE'D WEAKENED THE WALLS OF HIS PRISON! USING HIS...USING HIS..."

"...HIS HEAT VISION, HE CUT HIMSELF FREE!"

SUPER SANTA ACTION FIGURE

SANTA'S MAGIC SACK INCLUDED

NDER!! D SEPARATELY

"SANTA CLAUS DOESN'T HAVE HEAT VISION."

"WHO'S *TELLING* THIS STORY? ANYWAY..."

"...HE CUT HIMSELF *LOOSE*..."

"...AND OPENED HIMSELF UP A CAN OF WHOOP-ELF.

"HERE WAS A GUY WHO WAS USED TO COVERING THE *WORLD* IN ONE NIGHT.

"THE MAN COULD MOVE.

"HE WAS *GOOD,* FOR *GOODNESS'* SAKE.

"BUT IN THE END, HE WAS JUST *ONE MAN* AGAINST AN *INFINITE* HORDE OF HELL-SPAWNED DEMONS.

"IN THE END... HE FELL.

"AND
FA-WHOOM--

FA-WHOOM

"--NERON, UTTERLY
DEFEATED, DISAPPEARED IN
A VOLCANO OF FLAME--

"--LEAVING OLD
SAINT NICK TO
TURN THE LEAGUE
BACK TO NORMAL--

"--AND, IN TURN ACCEPT
OUR INVITATION FOR FULL
AND PERMANENT
MEMBERSHIP!

"AND THAT, MY FRIEND,
IS THE STORY OF HOW
SANTA CLAUS JOINED
THE JUSTICE LEAGUE
OF AMERICA!"

THERE. NOW WE'RE *BOTH* BELIEVERS, RIGHT?

YEAH! YEAH, I... ...I *GUESS*...

YOU *"GUESS"*? AFTER ALL *THAT,* YOU *"GUESS"*?

WELL, IT'S JUST... WELL, WHY WOULDN'T NERON JUST DO HIS *STUFF*? WHY WOULD HE *WARN* THE JLA AT *ALL*?

BE... BECAUSE...

AND HOW COME, IF YOU WERE IN *HELL,* THE MARTIAN MANHUNTER WASN'T HURT BY ALL THE *FIRE*?

I... THERE WAS...

AND HOW COME SANTA COULD TURN YOU *BACK* FROM *COAL* JUST BY WAVING HIS *HANDS*? AND HOW COME--

B-DEET B-DEET

A *SIGNAL CALL*! THANK *GOD*!

WHAT?

I MEAN--A *SIGNAL* CALL! *FOOEY*! GOTTA *RUN*!

RUN *AWAY,* YOU MEAN. YOU WERE PULLING MY LEG.

ME?

THEN *ANSWER* MY QUESTIONS!

I COULD--IF I HAD *TIME*-- BUT DUTY *CALLS,* PAL!

WE HAD A *DEAL,* REMEMBER? NOW GET SOME *SLEEP*! DREAM ABOUT *SKATEBOARDS* AND *VIDEO GAMES* AND JUST...

...BELIEVE...

THE STARS OF THE
DC UNIVERSE
CAN ALSO BE FOUND IN THESE BOOKS:

GRAPHIC NOVELS

ENEMY ACE: WAR IDYLL
George Pratt

THE FLASH: LIFE STORY OF THE FLASH
M. Waid/B. Augustyn/G. Kane/
J. Staton/T. Palmer

GREEN LANTERN: FEAR ITSELF
Ron Marz/Brad Parker

THE POWER OF SHAZAM!
Jerry Ordway

WONDER WOMAN: AMAZONIA
William Messner-Loebs/
Phil Winslade

COLLECTIONS

THE GREATEST 1950s STORIES EVER TOLD
Various writers and artists

THE GREATEST TEAM-UP STORIES EVER TOLD
Various writers and artists

AQUAMAN: TIME AND TIDE
Peter David/Kirk Jarvinen/
Brad Vancata

DC ONE MILLION
Various writers and artists

THE FINAL NIGHT
K. Kesel/S. Immonen/
J. Marzan/various

THE FLASH: BORN TO RUN
M. Waid/T. Peyer/G. LaRocque/
H. Ramos/various

GREEN LANTERN: A NEW DAWN
R. Marz/D. Banks/R. Tanghal/
various

GREEN LANTERN: BAPTISM OF FIRE
Ron Marz/Darryl Banks/
various

GREEN LANTERN: EMERALD KNIGHTS
Ron Marz/Darryl Banks/
various

HAWK & DOVE
Karl and Barbara Kesel/
Rob Liefeld

HITMAN
Garth Ennis/John McCrea

HITMAN: LOCAL HEROES
G. Ennis/J. McCrea/
C. Ezquerra/S. Pugh

HITMAN: TEN THOUSAND BULLETS
Garth Ennis/John McCrea

IMPULSE: RECKLESS YOUTH
Mark Waid/various

JACK KIRBY'S FOREVER PEOPLE
Jack Kirby/various

JACK KIRBY'S NEW GODS
Jack Kirby/various

JACK KIRBY'S MISTER MIRACLE
Jack Kirby/various

JUSTICE LEAGUE: A NEW BEGINNING
K. Giffen/J.M. DeMatteis/
K. Maguire/various

JUSTICE LEAGUE: A MIDSUMMER'S NIGHTMARE
M. Waid/F. Nicieza/J. Johnson/
D. Robertson/various

JLA: AMERICAN DREAMS
G. Morrison/H. Porter/J. Dell/
various

JLA: JUSTICE FOR ALL
G. Morrison/M. Waid/H. Porter/
J. Dell/various

JUSTICE LEAGUE OF AMERICA: THE NAIL
Alan Davis/Mark Farmer

JLA: NEW WORLD ORDER
Grant Morrison/
Howard Porter/John Dell

JLA: ROCK OF AGES
G. Morrison/H. Porter/J. Dell/
various

JLA: STRENGTH IN NUMBERS
G. Morrison/M. Waid/H. Porter/
J. Dell/various

JLA: WORLD WITHOUT GROWN-UPS
T. Dezago/T. Nauck/H. Ramos/
M. McKone/various

JLA/TITANS: THE TECHNIS IMPERATIVE
D. Grayson/P. Jimenez/
P. Pelletier/various

JLA: YEAR ONE
M. Waid/B. Augustyn/
B. Kitson/various

KINGDOM COME
Mark Waid/Alex Ross

LEGENDS: THE COLLECTED EDITION
J. Ostrander/L. Wein/J. Byrne/
K. Kesel

LOBO'S GREATEST HITS
Various writers and artists

LOBO: THE LAST CZARNIAN
Keith Giffen/Alan Grant/
Simon Bisley

LOBO'S BACK'S BACK
K. Giffen/A. Grant/S. Bisley/
C. Alamy

MANHUNTER: THE SPECIAL EDITION
Archie Goodwin/Walter Simonson

THE RAY: IN A BLAZE OF POWER
Jack C. Harris/Joe Quesada/
Art Nichols

THE SPECTRE: CRIMES AND PUNISHMENTS
John Ostrander/Tom Mandrake

STARMAN: SINS OF THE FATHER
James Robinson/Tony Harris/
Wade von Grawbadger

STARMAN: NIGHT AND DAY
James Robinson/Tony Harris/
Wade von Grawbadger

STARMAN: TIMES PAST
J. Robinson/O. Jimenez/
L. Weeks/various

STARMAN: A WICKED INCLINATION...
J. Robinson/T. Harris/
W. von Grawbadger/various

UNDERWORLD UNLEASHED
M. Waid/H. Porter/
P. Jimenez/various

WONDER WOMAN: THE CONTEST
William Messner-Loebs/
Mike Deodato, Jr.

WONDER WOMAN: SECOND GENESIS
John Byrne

WONDER WOMAN: LIFELINES
John Byrne

DC/MARVEL: CROSSOVER CLASSICS II
Various writers and artists

DC VERSUS MARVEL/ MARVEL VERSUS DC
R. Marz/P. David/D. Jurgens/
C. Castellini/various

THE AMALGAM AGE OF COMICS: THE DC COMICS COLLECTION
Various writers and artists

RETURN TO THE AMALGAM AGE OF COMICS: THE DC COMICS COLLECTION
Various writers and artists

OTHER COLLECTIONS OF INTEREST

CAMELOT 3000
Mike W. Barr/Brian Bolland/
various

RONIN
Frank Miller

WATCHMEN
Alan Moore/Dave Gibbons

ARCHIVE EDITIONS

THE FLASH ARCHIVES Volume 1
(FLASH COMICS 104, SHOWCASE
4, 8, 13, 14, THE FLASH 105-108)
J. Broome/C. Infantino/J. Giella/
various

THE FLASH ARCHIVES Volume 2
(THE FLASH 109-116)
J.Broome/C. Infantino/J. Giella/
various

GREEN LANTERN ARCHIVES Volume 1
(SHOWCASE 22-23,
GREEN LANTERN 1-5)

GREEN LANTERN ARCHIVES Volume 2
(GREEN LANTERN 6-13)
All by J. Broome/G. Kane/
J. Giella/various

SHAZAM ARCHIVES Volume 1
(WHIZ COMICS 2-15)

SHAZAM ARCHIVES Volume 2
(SPECIAL EDITION COMICS 1,
CAPTAIN MARVEL ADVENTURES 1,
WHIZ COMICS 15-20)
All by B. Parker/C.C. Beck/
J. Simon/J. Kirby/various

THE NEW TEEN TITANS Volume 1
(DC COMICS PRESENTS 26,
THE NEW TITANS 1-8)
Marv Wolfman/George Pérez/
various

TO FIND MORE COLLECTED EDITIONS AND MONTHLY COMIC BOOKS FROM DC COMICS,
CALL 1-888-COMIC BOOK FOR THE NEAREST COMICS SHOP OR GO TO YOUR LOCAL BOOK STORE.

Visit us at www.dccomics.com